The Sixties

A Forged Diary

John Crowley

Ninepin Press
Easthampton, MA

This is a work of fiction. All characters and events portrayed in this book are either fictitious or used fictitiously.

The Sixties: A Forged Diary copyright © 2024 by John Crowley. All rights reserved.

Ninepin Press
75 Clark Street
Easthampton, MA 01027
ninepinpress.com
info@ninepinpress.com

ISBN 978-0-9964220-5-5 (paperback) | ISBN 978-0-9964220-6-2 (ebook)

Printed in the United States on 100% recycled paper. Cover art: *Trompe-l'œil à la gravure de Sarrabat* (detail) by Jean Valette-Penot.

This book is one of four volumes comprising
John Crowley's Conway Miscellany.

Rain fell in my dream last night. This morning the streets are dry.

—Edward Weston, *Daybooks*

Introduction: Learning to Live With It

In the late days of 2021, caught at home as the Coronavirus raged, and having little to do beyond housework, I sought something to read that displayed a former world—perhaps a recent former world—and I picked up the first volume of Edmund Wilson's diaries. A neighbor, who had all three volumes and had decided he'd never open them, gave them to me. That was some time past, and for a while I supposed I'd never open them either. The first volume is *The Twenties* (Prohibition, New York, prostitutes, Vaudeville artists, Edna St. Vincent Millay, Scott and Zelda, and travels around the US). The great editor and biographer Leon Edel, twelve years younger than Wilson, assembled and annotated *The Twenties*, sometimes with only a brief note or identification *[Uncle Win, Winfield Kimball, a brother of EW's mother]* and sometimes a lengthy explanation. Wilson rarely gives dates, writes in a sort of shorthand, bits of things noticed, which is fun to read even when the people and their world aren't clear to the reader now. Other parts, with fewer obscure names and persons, are clear enough. New Orleans:

> *The green doors, blinds and walls of two-storied houses, all shuttered up, turned away from the street. Acorn scrolleries and exquisite laces of wrought iron balconies. . . . The smell of vetiver. The fragrance of raw sugar, like honey, like a fresher and sweeter molasses. . . . Myrtle, a very young prostitute. . . . She mocked a fellow—"Want your ass again? When you jazz last?" She had a guilty grin when I asked her if she liked her girlfriend a lot.*

After a hundred pages or so, I began to enjoy his rapid style and the clipped highlights and encounters, including a fair amount of sex, no euphemisms used except for humor. I am too old to keep a diary any longer (though I'm sure there are those who do), and I did write a lengthy record in the 70s—but what if I had chronicled my Twenties—which in my life would be the Sixties—in the manner of Wilson? His New York wasn't so different from mine—the Village, new movies, hippies, rock concerts, new thought, taxis, dope.

I kept no diaries or notes of my time in New York in the 1960s. But reading Wilson's, I thought perhaps I could write about those years now as I might have done then, in the way Wilson wrote his, on the fly. Not a memoir or a chronicle or an autobiography, dreary and endless, but an imaginary daybook: a sort of forgery, a forged version of an original that doesn't exist. I was not at the center, not even nearby, during many of the various explosions in the decade—of freedom or rage, the new art and the new film, war and resistance. I didn't yet understand myself or my talents, if that's what they were, when at length they began to make themselves plain. For this collection of days and nights I thought I should have an editor and annotator like Wilson's Leon Edel, though that figure would be imaginary too. His or their remarks and corrections would be set in italics within brackets, as Edel's are throughout *The Twenties*. They'd be brief, but my imagined critic or interlocutor would be granted a perspicuity I couldn't always dodge. I thought at times that he somewhat dislikes me.

In this account I can't cleave only to what I can believe I remember—not at the point in time I now approach, a *terminus ad quem*—nor can I entirely suppress the instinct to fantasticate that began to take hold of me as the new decade, marked with a 7, rolled in, somehow erasing the plausible and fairly gentle world I'd lived through and tumbling me forward into worlds I'd thought up without reckoning their strangeness, terror, glee, and otherness.

1963

[JC left his university in January, 1963, with a woman he was besotted with and who had, for reasons of her own, decided to leave school and move to California, and he went with her. She remained; he quite soon returned, alone. He stayed at home in Lafayette, Indiana, recovering from emotional breakdown and thoughts of suicide, and then in the fall he returned to the university, took up his studies, and completed the classes and projects he had left unfinished in the previous semesters. In August he left, not for Berkeley but for New York City.]

September. In Manhattan finally, after finishing the last class I took and will ever take at Indiana University. I am, except for the diploma, a college graduate. In my last week on campus I completed the photographing of the museum's small archaeological objects (coins, medals, carvings), the job that kept me in money all summer.

Today in a stationery store in the West Village I found a large thick book described on its face as a Record. What's to be recorded in the Record isn't specified, but it's a nice thing, generous pages lined in blue and with a red margin line. I thought it would have dates on the pages but it doesn't—I'll have to enter my own, if I care to. For me it will be a diary, I think, a record of this new phase/adventure/journey in the Great Oz that's New York City. And the first entry will be the story of my trip to Chinatown with the Pothead—yes, the same who'd brought marijuana to IU last year. He'd invited me to come stay with him then, and I've taken him up on it. Gave me a sleeping bag, and wakes me up each morning with a smoking pipe. Have thought it best to refrain—have to start looking for a job in photography or related field—did pound the pavements yesterday and the day before in the absurd suit I had inherited from Jim Riggs *[a graduate student at the university and friend of Lance Bird: see below]*. Right size but wrong affect, to no result.

Today the Pothead says we should rest up—go to Chinatown for lunch. Take the train. It's amazing—narrow streets, tiny restaurants, glossy smoked (?) chickens and ducks in the windows. The meal at the Pothead's favored place was like nothing I've ever eaten before. The walls were hung with paper menus or today's choices, all in Chinese. Waiters scurry from kitchen to tables with dishes. It was all magical, so cheap it might as well have been free, though likely the high-priced dishes weren't known to the Pothead—we settled for sweet-and-sour chicken, big lumps of deep-fried meat, dim sum, cheung fun rolls (the Pothead not quite sure what these are but they were tasty), and piles of rice. The Pothead gazing in delight at my delight. Back uptown in a daze—the Pothead notes (before falling asleep in the train) that everybody knows Chinese food makes you sleepy. We almost overshoot our stop, the Pothead clutching the lunch leftovers.

Lance *[Bird, JC's close friend at IU and his collaborator on a film project, never completed]* had told me I should go to a famed camera repair and sales shop he knows of, where a list of job openings or other opportunities for work is posted. Found the place—crowded with photographers getting repairs done or gabbing about equipment—news photographers with old flash cameras, others with Leicas, etc. Spoke to the owner about possible work. He asked if I had any studio experience—well, no, but I had worked in a museum photo lab. He flipped through some postings—"Here, Howell Conant Photography has a temp opening. Go work for him and come back and tell me you worked for Howell Conant." Which I will do.

Moved out from the sleeping bag at the Pothead's and gone to Carmine Street, Margo's apartment. I'm allowed to sleep on the couch tonight and maybe a couple more. Lance, who's technically Margo's boyfriend, who wooed her when he was last in NYC, hasn't yet told her when he'll arrive from Indiana. She's in thrall to Lance, I think. Much there still for him to deal with. Me, not so much. Couch was good for a week, and then she tells me that she has to give up the apartment for reasons I don't entirely follow, and offers it to me as a sublet (I think her parents have been paying her rent). Small, but pleasant; an elevator that I rarely use, nice kitchen and bath, nice West Village neighborhood. The current month is paid—but I have to have next month's in hand—$150. Don't know if I will be that flush by then.

Howell Conant Photography. A small large building—that is, large for its situation on an East Side dead end, but small enough to be manageable. Did NOT wear the Riggs Suit; jeans and jacket. Two photographers share the space, though the company is Howell Conant's. Major advertising and glamour photographer. The other partner shoots fashion for several clothing catalogues: knits, inexpensive dresses, sweater sets, etc. Place was overrun with tall beautiful young and not-so-young women. Don't stare. I got the job, which will be basically hauling equipment, doing what I'm told, and keeping quiet. I learned that Howell Conant was Grace Kelly's personal photographer. Huge blowups of her on the walls, some from *LIFE*, some more intimate. *[Howell Conant was the favored photographer of Grace Kelly and also the official photographer at the wedding of Grace and Prince Rainier of Monaco. Rumor had it that Kelly and Conant were briefly lovers.]*

JanR *[tall and blond, figured in the art film that JC and Bird spent much time on in their last months at college]* has arrived at Margo's; taking the bus for many hours from Indiana. She thinks—she's heard—that a cheap apartment on the Lower East Side is better than paying high rent on the West. Those Old Law tenements. Margo's horrified. You can't live over there—you'll get robbed—killed! Puerto Rican gangs. Black dope dealers! Sounds good to me. I'll get a *Village Voice* and go looking at rentals tomorrow. Lance—whose protégé Jan is, having starred as the Mysterious Beauty in *Tigers in Lavender*, the film we tried to make with inadequate equipment and no money—calls in to say that he thinks the LES apartment idea is just fine, and he and I ought to share one.

Saturday. Lovely vision after apartment-searching all day—stopping at Gems Spa on the Lower East Side—egg creams (which contain neither egg nor cream), *Daily News*, magazines, rolling papers, etc. I imagined this: two young men, peaceniks, who've dropped acid and on a stroll have come to Gems Spa for an egg cream. As one downs his, the acid hits, the scene is transformed; he learns that the other with him is an anarchist, and that he too might be one. . . .

The plot from then on is from Chesterton, *The Man Who Was Thursday*. It fits the present moment perfectly. Dreams of movie glory (but of movie creation more so). *[Nothing came of this conception, though JC harbored a fondness for the idea of a film taken from a book he put among the books he loved most.]*

Monday AM: Howell Conant. Trip out of town with Photog #2 for advertising photos (advertising is the mainstay of the operation, the movie-star portraits the glamour). Packed up equipment and drove in the studio station wagon out to a golf course in Seacliff, Long Island, an ad shoot for L&M cigarettes. Like climbing out of a dark underworld into sun and air. Gorgeous autumn foliage. Tedious foolishness of the ad: on the green, a golfer squats at the hole in open-mouth amazement to see a (female) hand rising from the hole, lifting a pack of L&M's. Where's the rest of her? In a dark dungeon below? Driven back to Manhattan along suburban roads lined with autumn oaks and maples under a dark blue sky.

Good news: an apartment on East 11th Street, in an Old Law tenement. Seventy dollars a month. First floor. Previous tenant of the apartment had put in some upgrades—the bathtub in the kitchen, which all Old Law apartments have, has a wooden wall to hide it, with a folding door to get access to the tub. Sort of unnecessary. Has a shower, though. Bed left by that previous tenant, in the front room with windows facing the street; another bedroom in the back. A "shotgun" apartment, open from front to back. Closest I've been to a person such as this, though many are to be seen—their ancient neighborhood. Neither I nor Lance, when he arrives, has much to bring in—clothes, cameras, books, furniture from the street. I'm loving it. Though soon to be attacked, knifed, and left for dead if Margo's right. No actual word so far from Lance. When I go by Carmine Street I find a letter from my mother (I'd given her Margo's address). The envelope includes a notice for me to report to the US Army draft board for assignment. Two weeks. I'd managed to get out of the first, or pre-induction physical, but this is final, though it doesn't read like it. I have to find a way out of it. I can't be a soldier.

JanR has decamped and gone east as planned—tiny closet of an apartment on East 3rd and Avenue D. Everything I had left at Margo's I pack in paper bags and a suitcase and take a cab to 7th Street and Avenue A. I give my wrinkled bills to the Orthodox Jew who's the landlord, or the landlord's employee, waiting for me at the tenement door. Brilliant and beautiful Puerto Rican teenage girls and boys. Girls sit on the tenement steps in the sun and watch the boys shoot at a basket attached to a garage wall. The boys show off, strut, mock, curse—*Coño, man!* The girls cheer and laugh at them. Half the block is out on the steps or in the street. Last summer days.

Exploring. Houston Street, northern boundary of the Lower East Side. Russ & Daughters bakery—floury, open space, wonderful odors of fresh bialys. Hoped to glimpse one or more of the daughters, but it seems they don't appear. Italian restaurant, a counter—most don't have that—where I order a plate of spaghetti and marinara sauce, which comes with bread; a glass—not a wineglass—of wine, all for 75 cents. Leave a dollar. Bialys for breakfast. Sign high on a building below Houston: IN THIS AGE

OF WOMEN'S LIB YOU'RE STILL IRONING HIS MAJESTY'S SHIRTS?!? And the name of a laundry.

Sunday. Went down to Wall Street for no particular reason. Vast silences, like a city of ice. A group of Asian sightseers overawed in the titanic empty canyons. Me too. Figured out how to get to Chinatown and had a meal in the same restaurant as with the Pothead, or an identical one. The food was just as good—but it wasn't quite as much fun to eat as it had been when stoned. *[JC's devotion to marijuana would continue, the only bar to daily usage being the cost, which though it sank rapidly in the years ahead, was still money, spent for grass and not for less spiritual sustenance. He refers in a letter to a moment when high, laughing in joy to feel "the old closed vaults" of his adolescence breaking open, the sources of his spirit in poetry, language, possibility.]*

New task at work: spot-toning. I had a vague idea how it's done—a very fine brush and an ink-like stuff called Spotone, diluted to a little lighter than the darker parts of the print. The job is to touch a brush laden with Spotone to any white dot or spot that's not part of the image and in this way delete it. There are always white spots from bits of matter on the negative, blocking tiny places on the printing paper. Black matter on a negative makes a white spot on a print. Tiring work, but I get good at it. Then, setup for a big ad shoot in the main studio tomorrow—this is Conant's bread and butter: big full-page color ads with people and sets and props that will run in the big magazines, *LIFE*, *Look*, etc. The studio boss—Jack—shows me a big double-page spread he worked on with Conant in Monaco: People sitting on the steps of the Monte Carlo casino in the early morning, reading newspapers; several in evening clothes, as though up all night; casino guards at ease. On the plaza a number of American cars, Ford models: they are what's being advertised. People are frozen in stance: valets opening doors, couples getting in. The casual morning light isn't chance—he wanted just this morning-after feel. It's lovely, even if it is just Fords.

PM: Getting the studio set up for the Thanksgiving shoot tomorrow. The lights for a shoot aren't basic studio lights—they're strobe lights, high up on stands. They're powered by thick cables running from batteries stacked in cases the size of a child's coffin. When Jack, Howell's top assistant, fires the strobe, it's a thud that hits your heart. This isn't Henry's classroom at IU *[JC and Bird studied under Henry Holmes Smith, noted photography teacher, at Indiana University]*. At closing time everybody gathers around a little bar and has a drink. Scotch or vodka. Jack makes himself a Martini. The janitor, a large man, has one too. And red wine for Howell's secretary Maggie, majordomo, bleach blond; the tall receptionist, recently a model, deep black hair cut in Vidal Sassoon geometric fashion by one of his New York epigones. And me. Howell has a couple and sends me out to get him a Mr. Goodbar for the drive home to Pound Ridge.

Friday night. Find my local bar: Stanley's, a block away up 12th Street to Avenue B. Sort of a Eugene O'Neill feel—dark and gloomy, lit mostly by ad posters and low lights. The hangout for leftists, argufiers, Marxists, advocates for various rights for various groups. Some names I know from *Ramparts* and the *Voice*. A new Bob Dylan song on the jukebox, played several times: *How does it feel, To be without a home, Like a complete unknown, Like a rolling stone* . . . Like being cherished and insulted at the same time. Bar shots are small and cheap, and easy to accumulate. Argument, or discussion, with political guy, finally I lose track and bid goodnight. Stagger back to 270, after momentarily forgetting the way, then to bed, only to awaken late to find I have vomited upward, over the wall, falling on the bed and my face. Never happened to me before. Disgusting.

After the laundromat and back with the clean things, walked over to the West Side to Margo's, pick up the last stuff I hadn't taken away. Another blue day, colder though. The trip from Avenue A and across Second to St. Mark's Place makes clear that the invasion that's been awaited has begun to arrive. Hippies, however the word is to be used—the thing itself obvious—litter the street or gather in clots, some barefoot, strumming guitars or blowing into penny whistles, holding out hands or hats for money; the whole pageant seeming to have been brought to life by newspapers and *Time Magazine* and TV. Cheerful, mostly. Imagine the trips some have taken from far parts of the continent. Montana, Missouri, Minnesota. Indiana, doubtless: a state easy to leave. Eye out for someone from the gang back at IU, though no ragged college sweatshirt gave a clue. Leaderless (so far). *Village Voice* pages discarded in a trash basket: *Baby Beatniks Spark Bar Boom on East Side*, where I am at present. A lot of these baby beatniks look too young to drink in bars.

Monday, a shoot in the big studio. The product advertised turns out to be Maxwell House coffee. Kitchen-table set with fake window lit from behind for yellow morning glow. Much moving of the camera and the people, out of Howell's hands at times as the admen seek ways to highlight the product. One young man with little to do (as am I) relates to me some of the secrets of advertising. The famed red Maxwell House can itself is too cluttered for an ad—the art department's created their own, the typeface not quite same or changed in size, and irrelevant information (price, guarantees) removed. Also I learn that the coffee itself that the actors lift to their mouths but don't drink isn't coffee but red wine, heated to give off visible steam. Real coffee is muddy and gray in a TV ad, but red shows as deep black. In the PM the food people work on the Thanksgiving set: plumping food with cardboard and paper to dispel a soggy look. The huge turkey won't be cut into. Couldn't it be cut up and handed around after the shoot? No. The real roasted turkey is given a coat of Vaseline or something similar for luscious glossiness. Ten family members (actors, kids and adults) around the table. All for the coffee.

Apartment near mine being emptied and the stuff sold—all piled on the street a block from my place. I bought a maroon leather armchair with tape on the arms but otherwise solid: one dollar. Carried it home and came back for more—a wicker chair with arms where those crosses of black had been woven in like a secret message or hieroglyphic—$0.50! Some burlap cloth I can maybe make curtains for the windows on the street, free.

Wednesday. Working in the upstairs studio with Roger and Harold Miller, photographer of the models for the pattern books: Sears catalogue, McCall's, Butterick, Spiegel. Famous models (not famous to me before, and many not famous to catalog buyers, mostly). Verushka is certainly famous, nine feet tall (seemingly) and with large long feet. I learned some first names—all that's needed. I asked Harold why these *Vogue* and *Bazaar* models come in and model these cheap dresses, and I got an answer: the big fashion mags mostly don't pay a lot. Models fight to get into them so as to be seen and be famous and "top," but the pattern books pay more, and a lot can be made per hour. Insider knowledge.

Full-fledged member of the Howell Conant team (for the time being). I'm allowed now to stay after the studio closes and take pictures and make prints. I can't use their cameras and strobes, but the standard lighting always remains up in the upstairs studio and can be hooked to my little Pentax. Having no model, I use myself: take all my clothes off and pose like a knotted and suffering Titan or fallen Victorian wrestler, with the remote cable to the shutter in my hand, hidden behind a leg. It worked. Somehow my slight body when contorted and tense seems large and muscular. Printed it on the studio's best 9x12 sheets of photo paper. When it was dry I rolled it up and slipped it into a tube taken from the trash. Train back downtown near midnight. *[This large photograph has disappeared along with many others over time; the only suggestion of what it looked like is a framed print hung on the wall of another Lower East Side apartment JC lived in later on.]*

JanR, who is beautiful beyond expressing, who doesn't love me but enjoys the company, has now moved into a nicer place, not far from the Conant place, oddly. She has acquired a monkey, brand unknown (to me), who shrieks and defecates in the usual fashion.

She's signing soon with a model agency, for which she's entirely suited except for lacking almost all real ambition in the game. On a night when I can stay late at Conant's, I take some pictures for her book—one in her glasses. They're good. They're free. She'll use them and maybe print my name on the ones I did. Small pleasures.

Next day was my trip down to 39 Whitehall Street to report for my physical and induction. Heart beating hard, I activated my plan. Because what I then did was actually a crime—though I'm fairly sure that mine will never come to light—I won't write down what I did to escape. Sufficient to say that a young homosexual like myself wasn't wanted in the US Armed Forces, and after a discussion with an Army psychiatrist I was allowed to go. Intense relief. *[JC's impersonation as homosexual was much more elaborate than this suggests—a willing or clueless psychiatrist he visited several times on the Upper West Side wrote a letter for JC noting his diagnosis of "possible schizophrenia" and also homosexual contacts, a fraud which could have had grave consequences if uncovered. It wasn't. And like all Vietnam War draft evaders, he would be pardoned by President Jimmy Carter in 1977.]*

Got a weekend's work for another photographer, near the Howell Conant studio. Notice posted in the photography newspaper—short-term assistant needed. His regular assistant had an accident, twisted ankle, and has to rest (all this communicated over the phone). I went over Saturday to meet him. Sort of the opposite of the Conant enterprise: a small apartment in a nice building, which he (his name's John Foote, a charming man) has turned into a studio—one bedroom, the living room his shooting space, the kitchen his darkroom (apparently he eats out almost entirely). Most of his work is headshots for models and actors, and he leaves the studio rarely—though what he needs this weekend is an assistant for a shoot at an apartment. The actress (I heard her name and sort of recognized it) wants to be shot in her own environment. So with him I carry the camera case and the lights across town in a cab and up an elevator. He uses a Hasselblad, a reflex camera I have only read about—the film is loaded into a magazine that attaches to the back of the camera. If you can afford them, you'd want to have two or three magazines loaded before a shoot so you don't have to reload. The only drawback to my eye is that all the images are square—you can't turn the camera sidewise from horizontal to vertical for two shots—has to all be done in the darkroom.

The starlet (not a name I recognized) was dark, sharp cheekbones, glowing blue eyes, and brilliant teeth. Seemed rather cold. Slim, almost skinny. She had a woman with her to help her into various outfits and check her makeup. Her apartment had few setups: on the white couch, in the negligee; in the bedroom, in the satin jammies; on the balcony, in the wide trousers; Miss Scarlet, in the library, with the candlestick. . . . A longish day. John, who does a lot of these, found her easy to shoot but unpleasant in looks when not smiling. We went to Brew's pub after putting away his equipment. I learned he'd been in the Army, and got a G.I. Bill loan that he spent on his studio setup, and that he's still paying off. I can't use that system.

Oddly, the next job I had with Howell and the B-team was photographing another apartment: Barbra Streisand's on Central

Park West, for *LIFE* magazine, a night job that ran in the end from 6PM to 1AM. Streisand not at home. Red brocade fabric wallpaper, Louis XVI antiques, baronial four-posters (more than one), pictures and posters building the myth. Some nice things, but the whole of it oppressive (a red brocade cozy for the television, e.g.). Overmuch, like the woman herself (my opinion). No sign of hubby Elliot Gould. Back home to 620 East 11th St., a different sort of place. And yet—I learned this today—she is the same age as me, born 1942. She seems much the older.

Margo has forwarded the letter from the Army containing my new draft card. 4F, or IVF in Army terms. Must be kept on the person and displayed to the appropriate officials at demand. Priceless. Do I feel like a traitor, a cheat, a sneak? No, I don't.

1964

Wonderful thing. Ran into L from IU, last saw her in the summer, before I headed west in January with Sandra Jean to California—where L is from. We'd had a night together off-campus—or most of a night, before she had to be in her dorm. Took me a moment to recognize her, but she knew me right away. She seemed glad to see me, even *very* glad, and I was glad as well, and we went to her apartment, which isn't much more than mine but is located just over the line in the West Village, and her bed is bigger and better than mine. I think we ate something, maybe drank something, and pretty soon it was morning, and there we still were. She's come to the city to seek her fortune—she'd like to work in advertising, and I said that I do work in advertising, in a way, and she should come with me to Conant's. Hope this continues.

Lance has at last arrived, bringing some rent money, camera equipment, great stories—some true, some outsized, some possible. He has a sheaf of contacts and is convinced that our college film-making can propel him upward. I listen to him talking on the corner pay phone (don't have a telephone yet): "You see, here at Wabash Films, we feel . . ." etc., as though a real office surrounded him. He's brought the poster for this imagined business that I made in the IU museum print shop. An ancient pufferbelly train, wood-block lettering—WABASH FILMS—and the motto: *L'acte gratuit*. Gave me a good feeling. Put it up on the wall.

A socialite (I don't think I've used that word before) came this afternoon to the shop. Her name is Jane Holzer, and I'm told she's married to a fabulously wealthy real estate magnate. Can't be more than a year or two older than me, though dwelling of course in realms beyond. Everybody in the shop very agreeable and just short of flattery, but she is ordinary enough in truth. Had a few headshots taken. I was told (after she left) that she's known around the Warhol world as "Baby" Jane Holzer. She has ambitions—modeling, films—and when she'd left the building, the staff here were not unkind.

And here's this—Baby Jane is going to appear tonight at a little club in the Village to sing and show herself to the world, and I—being the hip or hippie guy at Conant's—have been assigned to go down to this club and take pictures from the audience of her performing, for her uses. I've been given a Leica to use—my Pentax has insufficient stature. This looks to be interesting.

Well, it was, though not in the expected way. Baby Jane sang and twisted with aplomb and a friendly smile, and the audience, which surely came to cheer her, got things heated up. I was clicking away with the Leica from the third row when a guy leaned over to me and said, "Your lens cap is on." Which indeed it was, meaning that several poses hadn't been captured. I'm not used to a camera that's not a reflex—with the Pentax I'd have seen from the start that the lens was dark—but the Leica shows only what's seen through the viewfinder, so you have to assume you're taking that picture. Oh well. The actually fun part was the appearance of the Fugs in all their glory, Tuli Kupferberg, robed, on percussion—banging his jingle-jangle staff on the stage, reminding me of Garry Moore and *his* rattle-stick. They sang their hits, including "Bull Tongue Clit" and etc., but then they changed up; they sang in perfect country harmony William Blake's "How Sweet I Roam'd from Field to Field" as though it were a hymn, which it is in a tragic way. I might forget Baby Jane but I won't forget that.

Lance reproaches me at morning with the sounds L and I made in the midnight on my makeshift bed in the front room (he has the back). Kept him awake, he says, though I know for sure it isn't true. L thinks her apartment's the one for both of us, but the rent's higher and visitors are forbidden (who sets such a rule?). She's been coming to Conant's frequently, just to make herself known, and doing little tasks she insists on doing even without a payment. She's so cheerful and bright that everybody's going to help her up. Which gives me (this is baldly self-serving) a possible way out of the studio and into some beginning of my own work. But what *is* true is that I want to get a space where I can make photographs myself. All this being contingent on our staying together, which can of course never be known in advance, and only puzzled over after it does or doesn't. My history doesn't give any useful witness. Sandra Jean for whom I nearly killed myself. . . . No more about that here or anywhere.

Did a couple of nonpaying after-hours shoots in the upstairs studio at Conant's that maybe I can add to a portfolio: Nudes of a woman who wanted some to get work as an artist's model—on the heavy side and with a mass of black curls like a minatory Greek demigoddess—I shot her holding up a long spear (a curtain rod).

And a child model accompanied by mother. Pale, white-blond, large-eyed, unsmiling, sort of demonic actually. Sat her down on the seamless and placed a tipped-over cup and a spill of milk (cut from white paper; some sort of symbol I hadn't worked out and maybe couldn't). Mother hovering. "Can't you shoot some where she's smiling? She has a lovely smile." I don't want smiles, but I cooperate and take them "for her book," says Mum.

I have to have a studio space of my own if I'm going to become a photographer of people (am I that?). Look through the apartment/studio spaces in the *Voice*, etc. And here this morning is one listed that I actually might be able to afford, living and studio space combined, listed rent not impossible. Down in the old immigrant manufacturing district, which I've heard called Hell's Hundred Acres for all the factory fires in past times. The new term, apparently invented by a real estate developer, is SoHo—"south of Houston," get it? Most of those sweatshop clothing factories are now empty (which is why they burn). And whaddya know, when I arrived at the building with the space to rent—236 Lafayette Street—fire trucks and firemen and a cop or two are standing in the water from the hoses brought up the stairs. I ask who the landlord is—obviously it's the large man dressed like a janitor or super and surrounded by inspectors and fire officers. As I try to get his attention, I get an earful of the discussion—"Listen, Solly—c'mon—tell us—what were they doing up there? What set this off?" "I can't tell you a thing!" says Solly, a rich City accent. "The Cosa Nostra has sealed my lips!" They chuckle, roll eyes—must have heard this a lot. The fire's not serious, and is over now—open paint cans, etc.—and I'm allowed to go up, stepping over the hose at each floor. The third is the one that's for rent. I pass the john on the landing leading up to the space, which smells of smoke.

It's the most beautiful space I've seen in this city. No doubt there are a hundred more beautiful, but this one's mine, or will be mine, if I can get up two months' security. Solly (who maybe thinks this building is a source of trouble—the painter who started the fire is not in evidence) says he can wait for the security *"coupla weeks, no more"* if I've got the first month. Along both the long westward wall and the short southern wall are tall windows—four on the long wall, two on the short—probably eight feet tall. This was what I wanted: I can't afford lights, not good ones, but this place needs none. It's *natural light*, what Stieglitz and followers used. Of course my shoots (if any) will have to be on bright days. I feel the rumble of the subway, which has a stop at Spring Street, just outside this building. That we'll have to get used to.

A month's rent in advance, and two months' security, I can get that in two weeks with work at John Foote's and Conant's. I do a crude floor plan on a paper bag to send home to show them what I'm up to and ask for help. I'll be living and working here, and L will move in too, with expectations of marriage (this left out of letter as possibly evanescent). The wooden floor is splintery and rumpled, and in all the cracks are many metal snaps, the kind that were used in making clothes. The place was a sweatshop in former times. Maybe if I sit quietly for a long time I'll hear the sewing machines.

Solly walked me through the place by means of gesture. The fire alarms and sirens are constant, he says, but you don't care, you're an artist. Artists are all over my buildings. Some spaces are huge, this one's tiny. You see the kitchen? (A stove, a refrigerator, a sink). That's a plus, not all these have one, listen you don't use paint, do you? Chemicals, for photos? No sir—I'll process my pictures elsewhere. Solly is relieved. I ask him What about trash and garbage? Put it in the wire baskets on the street. What's the best time to put it out? After dark, says Solly, and hitches up his pants to get back to work. *[This famed landlord, his full name lost to history, rented lofts large and small to artists and others requiring large spaces. He flourished when the Artist in Residence (AIR) rule was passed in 1961, allowing qualified applicants to live and work in them. Solly (as JC terms him, probably inaccurately) appeared in an Andy Warhol art film of the late sixties with various art people. It's evident that he took pride in his renters and owners, and they in him.]*

So okay—I've been let go by Howell Conant Photography. Not enough work at the moment. You can't fire me, I quit! L however now has a part-time job there. But what she really wants—I don't know why—is to be a tour guide at the United Nations building. There are dozens of guides from many countries, she says—a *corps*, in fact. She's put in an application, and if accepted (whyever not?) she'll begin training. The studio gifts me with a roll of white seamless, not a full roll, in fact mostly gone. Jack drives me downtown in the studio truck with it bobbing in the back and helps me carry it up the four flights. He's rather taken with the place, wishes me luck.

Later I go out again to buy some lumber to make a platform bed. L hasn't *exactly* committed to living with me here, but the trend is toward yes, a little more every day.

———

The floor sanding and polishing went less well than I hoped. I helped the guy up the stairs with his sander and sandpaper and varnish. He seemed downcast: not used to such rumpled floors, perhaps; he wouldn't promise a high finish. I left him to it and set out on errands. When I returned a couple of hours later, he was finished but very annoyed. The floor was full of nails and metal objects (those snaps), and the old wood drank up the varnish thirstily, needing more coats. And one of the huge pieces of sandpaper that fitted into the sanding machine had hit a protrusion or a nail and ripped right down the middle. It had just been installed, brand new, he said. Expensive, he said. So I paid (what I had) for the extra varnish and the torn sandpaper and he left unmollified. The floor looks great to me. The whole place looks great to me. The Art Nouveau Mucha posters, the paper Japanese lantern-globe hung from the ceiling, the bed (which I had excluded from the job) all ready for the night. L gone all day at the UN being tried out or assayed or.

Late afternoon and a knock on the door. Beaky older man in a raincoat, fedora, briefcase. Seems to be surprised by me. Opens a packet of papers and reads out my address; he'd gone up to the floor above but was sent back down to here. Does L live here? Yes, I answer. And you as well? Um, yes. Her husband? No, no. Finally I invite him in and give him a seat, and I sit on the bed. He is an investigator for the United States Civil Service, which among many other things assesses Americans who seek positions in the United Nations New York facility.

He goes through some more paper and comes up with L's application. Also a notebook and pencil. Does L live here or does she visit? Lives here. With you? Yes. And your name is . . . Name supplied. He enters the name in his notebook. Seems baffled or defeated. Says gently but with an edge of censure that it's unlikely a young woman living in sin (not so stated but easy to guess) with a man not a relative or husband would be offered a position, he says. Certainly not common. Meanwhile I'm drawn to his argyle socks, which are drooping toward the ankles. Well, there's nothing more to say; he puts away his material in his ancient briefcase and his hat on his head and I show him out; she (L) will be, he says in farewell, sent a notice of the investigation.

I tell the tale to L on her return but she laughs it off—all her tests and her exams were fine, she was praised—*They LOVE me!* And in the next day's story that she brings back to Lafayette Street, pink-cheeked in the cold, blue eyes glittering—Yes, she got the job. Next week is her first day, and tonight we go to the Spanish restaurant on the West Side that's beautiful and good. She tells me (she's told me before) about her month in Lima, Peru, after high school, how she came to eat *ceviche*, raw fish in lemon juice baked in the sun; how she was once surrounded by scary young men who followed her with who knew what intentions, until she finally turned on them, bent over snarling and grunting, obviously mad—they left quickly.

L has told her parents that she's living alone in a new apartment and has given them the address to write to. But she's withholding the phone number—she's afraid they'll call when I'm here and she's not, and if I answer the call she is certain they'll learn of our *menage* and will do something drastic. So—with L's money—we've put in a second phone line, a phone only she will use, and is the phone her parents will call. After some discussion with New York Telephone we learn that each of the phones could have its own special ring (there are many to choose from). Now—unless we forget which phone is which—we will never be surprised. Phone #2 will never be rung except by the parents of L. (Of course neither phone is *ours*—both are leased by us from the company.) Thus the L-J pact is clinched, with that odd necessity.

She's sewing curtains at Conant's after hours to cover the bottom halves of the windows on the east side from neighbors' eyes (the building across Lafayette, at the border of Little Italy, where the boys on the roof play mumblety-peg or something more dangerous). We can also see, across Lafayette Street down Spring, a large Italian restaurant. It seems to be almost entirely empty, though an old grandma sits at the cash register that's stuck full of postcards from Italy. But instead of being the only two diners in that place, we go—L's idea—to the Paradox, a macrobiotic restaurant on 7th between First and Second Aves. Several long-haired males and females staring vaguely into space—something slightly threatening about that stare—with their bowls before them. The place requires a single waitress, because the dishes are basically all the same: "whole grain" brown rice, some vegetables unknown to me, and what my grandmother called "soya sauce," but this is different. A couple of boiled shrimp for the faint-hearted. L—who delights in unusual cookery and its variant healthy/delicious qualities, or the reverse, is good for it. I ate my bowl of rice willingly, foreseeing many further of the same. We also purchased an account of the health discoveries of George Oshawa, a Japanese theorist; the term "macrobiotics" is apparently his; L reading in it with great absorption; I soon drifted away from what seemed an impossible manner of life. *[George Oshawa died in 1966 aged 72 of a heart attack—though JC came upon other descriptions, or rumors, of death from stomach cancer.]*

A couple of small jobs at last. The receptionist at Conant's gets her hair cut at a salon on Madison that is the stand of a . . . now what's the word for a person who cuts women's hair?—A hairdresser, yes, who learned from Vidal Sassoon: the deep thick black straight hair like a helmet, the angled slash across the brow. She'll come here to have her picture taken after her new cut, and he'll put it up among his signature cuts, and maybe I'll get some trade from that. I have to find a photo house to develop and print.

Built a large closet thing, not very artfully but usable, found a cheap kitchen table and L brought kitchen utensils her mother had bought for her in her previous place. So, home sweet sort of home. We took stuff out to the wire baskets in the dark of night as directed and today went on the train to Brooklyn, where there's a Kroger's, the only grocery store within reach, and came back laughing with bags of groceries. L goes in Monday to start at the United Nations. She's searching through clothes that will make her look serious but cheery. There's a uniform you wear, she says. She had little interest in my own story of a uniform, ROTC back in Indiana, two semesters of marching and polishing brass.

Strange story about the Italian guardians of Spring Street. In a coffee shop I met two NYU grad-student women who had rented an apartment on the street and had got help moving in from a male student, also the boyfriend and soon to be fiancé of one of the two. So they'd been fixing up the place for a few days and sometimes having the fiancé over for dinner. Then they got a visitor, one of the black-suit guys, who had a concern. He made it plain to them that they couldn't conduct trade on their own, that they'd have to arrange a split with the neighborhood collectors. The girls were baffled—split what? With who? Well this guy we see, comes and goes. You working for him, right? That's not something we allow, tell you the truth. The women, finally getting it: No, no! He's this one's *fiancé*. We go to school, over at NYU. We just love this neighborhood! At last the enforcer gets it. They watch him blush, then pull himself together. Asks again: Really? True? Yes! Okay okay. I'm very sorry to insult you, it's my mistake, but it's understandable, right? And listen: You girls'll be okay. We'll watch out for you so nobody makes the same mistake. Okay? Anybody bothers you, just stop at the social club, next block, you'll find me. And he puts his hat on and leaves.

L says that any woman who's followed or threatened or feels scared in Little Italy can get help or protection by going into an Italian social club, the Ravenite on Mulberry street, the Knights of Alto on Sullivan, guys playing *Dama Italiana*, Italian checkers, true gentlemen.

We're learning the neighborhood. We've gone to the big restaurant on Spring (once)—we were the only customers, but the dinner was fine. Ancient waiter in dress coat, dishes very classic (says L who knows more about Italian food than me). The solemnity and silence were a little oppressive. On Sundays, though, black limousines show up on the block, men in black go into the restaurant, the street remains blocked with Cadillacs, drivers at the wheel, nobody taking exception to this. We decide that they come in from Queens or Brooklyn for meetings and pasta, take the parents still living on the block to church or dinner. From out our windows we can see them come and go.

1965

My old chum Dan McC, former seminarian (briefly), boyfriend (briefly) of my sister Kathy, has moved to NY. *[Daniel McCauslin entered the Holy Cross Seminary in South Bend as a ninth grader and remained in the novitiate until he left in his third year; thereafter a student at St. Joseph's High School, where JC was a student.]* He's brought his wife and two young boys, not more than two or three years old I'd guess. I was at the wedding, in South Bend. Good to see him. Still crew-cut and short—as short as me, black-rimmed glasses. He worked at the newspaper that served Mishawaka, South Bend's Sister City as it is somewhat deviously named. Now he's getting a job with the Liberation News Service, which couldn't be more different from the square and sleepy Mish *Times*. I don't know when he got to be a leftie, but South Bend was always a union town—Studebaker, Bendix, etc. L likes him too. We're going to take him places (the wife 'n' kids are setting up in an Upper West Side apartment—he must have got a nice severance payout).

Sunday on the Staten Island Ferry, the three of us. World's cheapest ocean cruise—one nickel, though about to go up. Running through the terminal to get the next departure, passed a newsstand managed by a loud and angry man in black. *Hey, Chump! They got you fooled! The Beatles made the money! Ha! Look like a dope! Too late, suckers!* We didn't stop to explain to him that we hadn't, or wouldn't have, grown Beatle cuts for the money. Anyway, laughing, we got on board and out into the bay and Hart

Crane's seagull's wings that "dip and pivot him, shedding white rings of tumult, building high over the chained bay waters Liberty"—couldn't resist. And they really do shed white rings of tumult, but more tumultuous over the garbage barges. Brilliant air and sun. When the big tub pulls in shouldering the huge black pilings aside (or seeming to), there's nothing more to do but cross over and pay another nickel to get back. Quieter, the three of us on the way back, maybe thinking, what's to become of us.

Quite coincidentally sister Kathy came to New York for the fun of it. I'd given her the address, and she found the place easily. Dan McC is here, but L is at work. The first thing my mathematical sister did was to pose a question. What defines the progress of the following numbers, she asks: 59, 50, 42, 34, 23, 14, 4? Dan and I muddle over this for a while, asking for hints, dividing and multiplying. Dan, who just got here, had no reason to get this puzzle, but I'm ashamed that I didn't: not a math puzzle, not a trick—just the numbers of the subway stations' streets, which she'd memorized, from 59th to 4th—the last before Spring. Of course. The two of them renewed acquaintance, or whatever it might be called; they started quoting Johnny Carson's continuing jokes on *The Tonight Show*, leaving me out—I'd never seen the show (no TV) and knew nothing about him, but they could tie one ringer of his to another for quite a stretch.

Sunday afternoon. Go alone to Bleecker Street Cinema to see *Sins of the Fleshapoids*, the Kuchar brothers film that Andrew Sarris calls a "science fiction film," a phrase so unlike the film described as to mean nothing. "The TIME is a MILLION YEARS in the FUTURE," a voice cries. The film is astonishing. I think about these films (they were also showing Maya Deren's *Meshes of the Afternoon*) as if the contents were actually produced in the bodies of the producer-director-actor-dancer and released into the space, coalescing in color and sound. The glaring Kodachrome of *Fleshapoids* is perfect. The set—velvet fainting couch, ransacked bureau littered with candy bars and cellophane bags of potato chips, is also perfect. The sort of flying-saucer cast-cement pod of *Fleshapoids* and the Mediterranean sandy-white battlements of *Meshes* are equally summoned up by will. *Meshes* bored—Maya in white robe wandering barefoot, touching white walls in the sun, in Spain or somewhere, etc.

Hired back at Conant's for a day or two. *LIFE* is to do a big fashion spread and wants to have "underground" movies as backgrounds, more specifically movies made in the Warhol Factory. Conant seems to think I have some sort of connection with art movies and similar way-out stuff that in fact I don't—though for sure I know more about Jack Smith's wild *ouvre Flaming Creatures,* and somewhere with Lance I'd met Andy's film guy Gerard Malanga—he produced lots of short sex films (*Blow Job*, etc.) and also that stream of films that last for hours in which nothing happens. *LIFE* has some opinions about which of these they want as backgrounds and which ones they *don't* want. Some of this has already been negotiated when I go uptown to pick up the cans of film and taxi back to the shop. Long wait in an office chair observing the Factory doings. Andy stops by to find out who I am, and we have a momentary meet before he evaporates. *[Three years later in the Factory, Warhol was shot and nearly killed by Valerie Solanas, who felt that Warhol had rejected her and her work; JC remembers her passing through on one of the trips to the Factory in 1965.]*

Following day, a 16mm projector set up and the women of *LIFE*—producers, editors, art directors, chiefs of fashion and publicity—go through the various offerings. A screen had to be set up large enough for the models, and it didn't work—its mechanics showed in the shot—so the widest seamless white paper was used instead. The Warhol mode of endless hours of a sleeping person or a static building (*Sleep*, John Giorno asleep, some 5 hours long, and *Empire*, the Empire State building seen through a window, 8 hours long). Others were screened, but they had too much begowned boy-sex in them, or at least suggested. The ladies perked up at *Flaming Creatures*, which had been let out of movie jail last year after Susan Sontag and Jonas Mekas intervened. 80% or more of the film was drag queens, smeary lipstick kisses, enveloping gowns to trip on, wide-eyed madwomen, operatic death scenes, and lots of obscene dialogue that wouldn't matter because the *LIFE* shoot could only be still pictures. The big decisions that had to be made were about which model in which clothes would be shot with the Creatures gesticulating around her, with unknown intentions. One model in deep-green silk stood with the projected unmoving body of Giorno, bent over him as though to place a fairy kiss on his brow (at least one take looked like that; less freaky posing followed). Howell kept his council, allowing himself to be in second place. I thought—but couldn't say—that *Sins of the Fleshapoids* would have been much better as background—and in color.

Later on, a cocktail gathering for participants, with further movies projected and Andy and others present, his movie star Joe

Dalessandro, Gerard, more. I was close enough to hear a conversation between two *LIFE* women. One whispered to the other that she just *had* to talk to Andy—bring him down a little . . . I followed in her train as she wound through the crowd, and when she got Andy's attention I was close enough to hear this conversation:

SHE: Andy! I have something you'll love—a funny thing about the Supermarket Art show—you know?
WARHOL: Oh yes. That was fun.
SHE: Yes! I bought something from the "Meats" case—wasn't that by Wesselmann?
HE: Oh, I think so, yes, I guess it was. That's wonderful.
SHE: Yes, and I also bought a bag! *[Purchases of Supermarket artworks were put into brown paper grocery bags for purchasers, each bag signed by Warhol and others. The bags cost $50.]*
HE: Oh yes, that was so fun.
SHE: Yes but, here's the story. I took the bag home, and my son, who's ten, found it and put his books for school in it . . .
HE (almost animated): Oh wonderful, that's wonderful.
SHE (laughing): But but . . . the bag broke on the way to school! It was a crummy bag!
HE (moved): Oh that is so . . . Oh come here, you must tell this to [name missed], it's wonderful.
SHE (now seeming to think it was maybe not all that funny): Well, of course he didn't know what it was, or how valuable . . .

I could tell she was a bit nonplussed by Andy's reaction, but he wasn't being dismissive or impatient with her, he just thought it was a great story about the whims of art. Which it is.

Soon I was back home on Lafayette Street, a little drunk, and found my UN Tour Guide studying her lessons. Let's put those aside just for now, hey, said I. Told her about the craziness at Conant's. Then she changed into her jammies and got under the covers—but a bed without a backrest is hard to hang out in. Beautiful small perfect body she has. Her former and maybe only boyfriend, back in college, was an athlete—bicycle racing, the Hoosier sport—and was a poet and also a controlling and oppressive bully. She was often afraid in the earlier days in NY that he'd show up again; I was to protect and defend (spiritually) and win back her self-certainty. Which I think I did. And yet there's a part of her that kept her with or under him for a long time. She seems to wait sometimes for me to take up that role, maybe just in games, but in games that I fail at. Cruelty, even the pretend kind, might be her thing but isn't mine. She's not my prisoner (am I hers?). *[The writer and cyclist was Steve Tesich, who also came to New York after graduation. He was the author of plays and film scripts, winning many awards. He died in 1996 at the age of 53. For all that JC learned about him, the two never met.]*

Getting colder. L and the *corps* at the UN were approached by a guy selling warm coats—rabbit fur dyed to look like lynx. L, who shivers a lot, put in for one. The idea of bunny made to look like lynx I find neat. And now she'll be warm. November starts tomorrow.

Nine days later. I'm up on Lexington Avenue after working an afternoon with John Foote and his assistant Richard. About when we're thinking of going to Brew's pub, the day suddenly darkens. Foote's lights shuddered and went pale, flickering on and off.

Something in his building shorting out. Then we went to the only window in his place that showed the streets—and the lights in buildings were shutting down. Then the streetlights. Ah, nothing—they came back on. Then off again and not on. It was now dark in Foote's place so I headed down the street to Conant's and met L coming up. We walked down Lexington: people with flashlights, people gathered around other people holding transistor radios: the power is going out all over the Northeast, from Canada and Vermont west to Buffalo and Albany and as far east as Boston. We all said that we'd never seen a blackout like this one. Then said it again. We wondered if the trains were stopped, and what about the people already on them, rush hour, what then? And—wonderful—looking east along 52nd Street, out in the sky to the east, a big yellow full moon. By the time we walked as far as 34th Street you could see by it. The silence (subway roar under the street extinguished) and stillness. It took a long time. Still total dark when we reached 236 Lafayette. Only lights on were in the huge police headquarters a block downtown on Centre Street. Sirens call-and-response. Time for bed.

Another Conant temp gig: we need the money. *LIFE* magazine again, for which Howell has done so much work, assigned him a double-page (triple-page?) layout featuring three up-and-coming female stars next week. It'll take all day.

It did take all day. The three up-and-comers are Claudia Cardinale, Raquel Welch, and another whose name I heard spoken several times but damn can't remember it now a day later. Vanessa? Raquel was the least personable and the one with the least of that mystic force of soul—need—power—can't think of the word that means what these people have. Her big movie, *One Million Years B.C.*, mixing cave people and dinosaurs, looks ridiculous in the posters, but the boys are swooning, I guess—in person I didn't think she was actually sexy; as though she expressed sexy but didn't feel it. She didn't like the clothes chosen for the shoot (I'm thinking that nobody suggested a cave-bear skin and a spear). She felt unsteady in heels on a sawhorse-plank setup, and too much makeup (I think many women wear too much makeup).

Vanessa (?) didn't seem to have much sex force either, though she was very nice—seemed like a Sarah Lawrence or Bennington girl. Dressed in a modest skirt and sweater, and in one setup a raincoat. But Claudia Cardinale was wonderful. She exudes sex but seems to be unconscious of it; she's small, shorter than me, but she has an open expression, dark wide-spaced eyes, a smile even when not smiling (yes, it's so). I got to stand with her for a while—I worked the fan that made her hair move. I did it well. She smiled at me. She THANKED me! Speaks basically no English. She had an Italian press-relations team and an aide or overseer, also tiny and smiling; when Claudia went into a makeshift dressing room to change, he'd check his watch, smile, go knock at the dressing-room door gently and call in delicately—*Clowdia* . . . until she came out. I haven't been and likely never will again be that close to a real movie star, and mine was a very nice and very, very . . . sexy one. Was it a gift of time? Was I lucky? I look at my fellow males and try to guess if within them they have the same instant upsurge of . . . well, what is it, lust of course but not only, a sort of step into a realm where my actual person takes place and the reason for it is known. Are they—other guys—commanded as I am, or are they mostly placid or competitive or caught up in the things they know how to do? If they *are* commanded, is the feeling of it the same for them as for me?

Lance has made a darkroom in an outbuilding attached to his and Betsy's building in Chelsea. [*Lance Bird had developed a relationship with a woman, Elizabeth Lindley, from a wealthy family in Rye, New York. Elizabeth (Betsy) had not long before broken off a difficult relationship with the Polish writer Jersy Kosiński, and though they were still friends, Lance wooed and won her.*] I've been developing there, large but not huge photos of the women I've photographed, but done in various dark settings and in various dark Arts and Crafts or Pre-Raphaelite clothes that they've chosen. Some come from pictures taken in Bloomington. Some have that calm assessing regard of the first generation of women who found they could meet the forthright assessing regard of men: what I aimed for. I've also worked out a stamp—not an actual stamp, but the form of a stamp of the kind that artists around 1900, including Whistler, used on their paper works—sort of Japanese styling. I like what I have made. I'm actually building a portfolio, something I've never achieved—large and good enough to bring to the magazines.

Couple more pictures made in Lance's place, including two that were made by a "gum-print" process described in a book that I discovered in a junk shop. Make an emulsion by mixing water, gum arabic (sticky), ammonium or potassium dichromate and a dry watercolor pigment, and coat a sheet of plain art paper, smooth or slightly rough, cotton fiber with some "tooth." I used a blue-green. I thought it would be hard to find a light-sensitive medium, but the dichromate required (poisonous) was easy to get. When the coated paper is dry, use a photograph, printed on thin photo paper, as a negative. Place this face down on the coated art paper and expose in sunlight. (I had a piece of glass that could be laid on the two sheets.) When fully exposed—it's a guess—take the colored sheet and slip it into a bath of warm water. Where the dichromate was exposed to the sun it will be permanent when dry, but as it sits in the bath you can use a paintbrush to thin or even brush away parts of the image. Lovely, delicate images, evanescent-seeming but when printed on strong art paper actually very tough—won't fade away. Surely no one in the fashion business is making gum-print images. I'm so pleased. Those two students that I photographed with the big camera my last year in college—pale and serene, like Victorian sisters—those negs are what I'm working with now.

Monday. Choices. Filled a large portfolio, then took out one or two, then put them back in, plus another. Pictures from Conant, including the naked male figure (me) and a crazy thing made from an Ektachrome slide—John Foote was out of his studio that day, and his handsome assistant Richard helped us with a background Foote uses a lot, a sort of oil-portrait look. We included Richard's girlfriend swathed in white, another guy they brought shirtless and raising a chalice. Sort of like a frame from *Flaming Creatures*. Then I blew up the slide in a Conant enlarger and muddled it up to look like an 1890 big-camera colored print. Then applied my stamp.

Deliver entirety to the art department at *Harper's Bazaar*. They want "young" and "now" and "groundbreaking"—I can't say if that's what I have given them. They will let me know when they've looked it over and I can return. The current *Harper's* look is not so far off from what I was pursuing—Janis Joplin, hippie costumery, long sweep of hair, minimal makeup, lost girls, crazy girls, ghosts of the '20s. When summoned I'll bring more of what I brought before.

That summons comes quick, which suggests what? Get this crap out of here? I travel uptown to the Hearst Tower and get into the first elevator going up to the layout floor. Standing beside me as we whiz upward, I realize, is Richard Avedon, on his way to the same offices. We enter the great premises together; I stand far back and watch the interchange between Avedon and Nancy White. A whole new look: space travel. Models in space suits and space helmets. Here's Jean Shrimpton, Avedon's creation, in a white space helmet. Moonscapes, stony heights, spaceship interiors, glossy and plastic.

I am eventually noticed and sent away to talk to a lesser person about my submission. It doesn't go well. This was not the time for what I thought I could do, even if I did it well—which the boss here seemed to think I hadn't, and all the young women gathered around her also thought not. *You know, just because you put a STAMP on a photograph doesn't make it ART.* Nods all around. It all lasted about ten minutes, one or two grudging compliments. The talk returning to space, Shrimpton, and Avedon, as I was escorted out with my portfolio.

Coming on top of this, on returning to Lafayette Street L tells me she's pregnant.

It's absurd to think of ourselves as parents. She is clear on that and on the necessity of getting over what's started as soon as possible. It can't be very late in the process—we've been chaste in the last month, for the various reasons couples do become chaste in stretches, which can be all right or can be poisonous. I've asked her how long it's been, how far along, and she's got the start-point figured out at least. She's entirely clear that I am the male in question, and I believe her. I ask how she learned about the condition: from a drugstore, she said. It's not hard. But she hadn't told me she was even worried about this, and hadn't said anything. I thought we'd been careful. One incident of *coitus interruptus* or quick-draw; maybe a little leakage. All that's necessary is one little thrashing sperm. Next thing now is to find a way to end this. L says she has some way to get a doctor. They exist. They also charge, and lots.

Very quiet and emotionally dark at 236 Lafayette. I can't tell if she's angry with me.

It's the UN Tour Guide corps, or rather their overseer, supervisor—never been sure of the title—who has the information. And the sympathy; more than one of her international company of girls has needed it. Imagine having to go back to India or Russia or Turkey with this problem unsolved. L says that the doctor she knows is a good man and a kind one, but really does that matter, she wonders—what really matters is that it will cost $200, which has to be got, in cash and soon. Careful negotiations with families, loans asked for to pay imaginary needs. Thinking of what we could sell. Nothing I can see. I called Lance, who has gotten backing for his stock-car-racing movie; I asked if I could get an advance on the writing I had been assigned to do for the film. He thought he could get me fifty. At the end of the week we were almost meeting the $200 limit. Now L has got her paycheck. We have an appointment. I'm wondering how this will affect our bond, or relationship—if we even have one now.

The doctor—a real doctor, according to the buzz around the Tour Guide corps (what have they all been up to?)—has his office on First Avenue, a few blocks south of the United Nations building. We arrive early. She's holding the $200 in an envelope that had held a letter from her parents. I'm admitted to the waiting room, but L almost immediately sends me away. It's a cold day but bright. I leave the building, find a nice bench (First Ave is more upscale in this neighborhood than I knew) with a view of the door of the doctor's building. Sat. Waited. Smoked a few cigs. And there she was, exiting the office, not knowing which way to turn, not seeing me. I reached her; she was pale, red-eyed, calm. I took her arm and she allowed that. I got a taxi, and we went back to Lafayette Street. I wanted to ask questions but I felt sure she wouldn't answer, not yet at least. She was hurting by the time we got to the building; walking up the stairs hurt. The doctor had told her it was going to be a rough day and night. She got to the toilet in the landing and went in and shut the door.

When she could talk—wrapped in a blanket, lying on the bed, pillows around her—she said the doctor was kind and gentle, maybe a bit judgmental—scolded her not about sin, just carelessness. She'd get off the bed every few minutes, wrap the blanket around herself, and head again to the john. I could hear the moans or groans. Then, finally silence. The toilet flushed, and again, and once more. *It's what he told me,* she said. *That it was going to be painful and it was going to to hurt, not the pain, but the heart.* I made tea and she drank it, holding the cup in both hands. Handed it back to me and cried some more, softly. I thought how women can cry bravely, or strongly, in anger or pain. I can't. Men can't, I think.

It was over, she judged, and took a pain pill the doctor had given her, and lay down on her side, legs drawn up like a child. She let me cover her with the blankets. I read for a while till I was sure she was fast asleep and slipped in beside her.

This morning she's herself again, mostly. She showed me the birth control pills the doctor had given her in their toy container, and a prescription for more. *Now it's going to be okay,* she said. I begin watching her every morning, naked or in a shift, carefully dialing the disk to the next pill and popping it out.

1966

New tenant at 236 Lafayette. L, out walking; a Puerto Rican boy came up to her, holding a cat. Hey, lady, want to buy this cat? No, she didn't, and the cat was battered and filthy. *Coño*, lady! It's a good cat! Okay, for nothing. *Nada*. Take it, okay? And she did. The cat's here now, and so far okay with the place and ourselves. Brushed and petted now. L has given her (it's a her) the name Mao. "Cat" in Chinese. Like Mao Tse-tung. Sort of lovely, actually: each meowing in their own way. This surely has a string from the abortion attached.

Meeting artists and other photographers who are moving into the SoHo lofts, some of them enormous. The AIR rule that Mayor Wagner signed before I arrived in the city, "Artist in Residence" signs on loft doorways so emergency vehicles can see that people might be in the buildings (most of which have been empty since the end of small manufacturing in Manhattan). Mine is probably as small as they get. The painter in the space above us has room for big canvases (he's painting Marvel Comics characters in bold colors). L met a painter with a loft on the other side of West Broadway, the bare and desolate street one over from Lafayette. We had him over for a drink. Handsome guy, in a sort of black-Irish way. When he'd gone she told me he'd asked if she'd model for him. Can't argue—she's modeled plenty for me.

Landed a new job—this one in the art department of an outfit called The Radio Advertising Bureau, whose goal is to increase advertising on the radio. If I understood right at the intake, they are funded by a consortium of radio stations, big ones and small ones, or Large Markets and Smaller Markets, seeking ad revenue. I'm to make posters, do studio work, take photographs for their advertising, etc. A smart guy shares the small space with me—a real commercial artist—and teaches me stuff. Also from the library I got a book called "Commercial Art and Studio Skills," which I have committed to memory. I worried about my skills: how to use a drafting pen, which makes a perfect line of any of a number of widths when set up correctly. But the guy—I think of him as my boss—showed me that the drafting pen I thought I'd have to learn to use was passé, and what was used now was black tape, in many sizes thin to thick—just run it off like a mini Scotch tape dispenser, and there's your line. He also taught me how to do a complex layout—cover a card with rubber cement, then lay down the text pieces and the pictures, etc., and then when it's done take a hunk of dried rubber cement and gently but firmly rub the card, which will pick up all the excess rubber cement, and with it all the fingerprints and other marks, into a larger hunk, leaving a perfectly clean pasteup. This process was extremely pleasing. Watching him at work is a delight. I'm learning a lot. Lance wants me to make a poster for his new idea—a documentary about the huge TT ("Tourist Trophy") motorcycle races on the Isle of Man. The poster's great. Lance seems to feel that a great poster can make a great film, or draw the funding for one. The races are far off. *[Neither JC nor Bird ever reached the Isle of Man and the TT races.]*

First RAB assignment with the camera is to take pictures of people listening to radios—transistor radios on the street, not hard to catch at Los Lobos; car radios—harder to set up with a willing stranger—and desk radios, one of them my own, tuned by L as I took her picture. Supposedly all candid but all of them posed. Radio is everywhere! I had been given a roll of Kodachrome to use also, but candid color is hard. What I spent the roll on was L: half-undressed, naked, displayed, smiling. Have to find someplace to get these developed as slides without the photo house noticing what they are and discarding them. It's happened once before to me and often to others.

The RAB (Radio Advertising Bureau) is housed in a pretty little mansion just off Madison Avenue in the 50s. It seems to be a sort of minimal enterprise. The salesmen are long-standing, dropping by the art department just to talk, or to imagine pictures or sales tools we might work up. Last week it was an oversized imitation hundred-dollar bill, with David, the Director's, face in the oval instead of Franklin's. I'm not sure what function this was to have, but I did a nice job with the machines in the art department. When the test prints were passed around, though, one of the execs came to me somewhat alarmed. Why had I made the Director's nose so large? Was I doing this as some kind of joke? If it is, it isn't funny. It took me a while to realize that he thought I'd made a Jewish caricature out of the Director—wasn't it obvious? Not to me; however much I'd become a New Yorker, this common insult had *not* occurred to me. I didn't know that David—the Director—was

Jewish, and how would I? The exec was mollified but I had to redo the print job.

What day was it—maybe Saturday—we were coming back from the Brooklyn Kroger's, and we get offered another cat. This one tiny, maybe days or weeks old, white mostly with black patches. Do we want another cat? I've never had even one before, but I like them. And this one so desperate. So we take her home—thinking we can remove her later—and here they both are now. Mao's hissing and teeth display had no effect on the new one (who has been named Punky for no reason I know, not my choice), maybe too young to notice a threat. She spends a lot of time licking at and pressing her mouth against the tiny pink teats she sees. She nuzzles until she's exhausted. Hard not to feel for her. I thought of the doctor on First Avenue, and the aftermath.

July. Our acid trip. A couple of sugar cubes with a drop of the magic fluid on each. In the context of this life we're all living, it was a disappointment. We hadn't followed the instructions of gurus that you should clean your premises, wash your body, meditate before taking off. We didn't follow that advice because we hadn't heard it. Too bad, because the first thing that hit was an overwhelming lust we both felt, clinging and panting together standing up—but then L drew away—the idea of falling onto our messy bed at 9AM turned her off. The rest of the day was simply odd: walking in the neighborhood, a sense of prickles of electricity in the air, a shifting, glassy vision of buildings; nothing was revealed. Maybe it wasn't even LSD we took. L's responses were more interesting (to her) than mine were to me. Oh well.

October. Quit the Radio Advertising Bureau. (My buddy in the art department had left already, and his replacement was no one I wanted to spend all day with). I finished a set of 35mm slides that would replace the stodgy old sales pitches on paper. The slides were good—colorful, expressive. I'm out. David (whose nose is perfectly ordinary) invited me up to his office for a talk—asked if I could stay—fine job I was doing. The office had obviously once been a rather magnificent bedroom, with bathroom and large closets with dark-wood doors. And no, I said, I was going back to school to get a master's degree in art. He waved me away.

Jack at Howell Conant's had sent me to a photo shop he goes to that does color developing and doesn't care what the slides show—so long as it's not a crime scene. Certainly the secretary made no comment silent or otherwise when I came to pick them up, all 36, neatly sealed in their plastic box. A slide projector previously loaned to me by the RAB, which of course I might certainly maybe return. We lay together on the bed and projected her beautiful self onto the seamless, pictures four or five feet wide. Her perfect breasts. One pic she didn't recognize: a closeup of her pubic hair, like a stand of dry grasses at the edge of a pale savannah. We left the projector to cycle through the pictures while we.

A week later. Went to an afternoon screening of *Alphaville* with Lance. L had no interest in the movie or in the inevitable discussion between Lance and me about the film and said she'd do errands. I returned late afternoon, surprised to find L there, bright-eyed and elated. She'd spent the afternoon with her painter. Yes, she'd modeled for him. Yes, they had sex. Just a thing, she says to me: a crazy thing. Waits for my response; sits silent on the bed, watching. But I have nothing to do or say. And she has nothing more to add.

Later in that week L tells me she's decided to go stay with Dan McC in his apartment. Not the one with the wife and kids in it but the one with just him. To try it out. This was extraordinarily painful. That painter guy was unknown to me, but this was an old friend; I was a member of his Indiana wedding. But somehow I don't have the energy or force or whatever it is to rage at her. Couldn't even if I could. A sort of cold stasis settles over me that probably seems like acquiescence or nonintervention. But it's not that. She lies beside me sleepless that night (but sleeps in the end; not me though). I think I see—maybe just sense—that's she's crying in the morning as she packs stuff. She hugs me as she goes out the door. Nothing said about the future. Maybe she sensed failure in me. That had surely been the case with Sandra Jean.

[Sandra Jean Love, whose father, William Love, was an executive at Studebaker in South Bend; she'd started at Indiana University in the same year as JC. They met late in the fall semester of 1963 and embarked on an intense (for JC; Sandy had had previous lovers) romance. At the semester's end, JC signed up for an intra-semester course, and with all dorms closed he could settle in with her in a tiny apartment in town. When the semester was to begin, they weren't allowed to stay in the apartment, and Sandy would have to return to the dormitory. That was

the impetus to quit school and go west. JC has, in general, been a follower not a commander in love.] I don't have enough experience—hardly any—but it seems to me possible that women have, or can have, a sudden impulse to go: to drop one scene and create another with another guy, without a look backward and without any sense of guilt beyond a tear or two. Of course in song and story it's the man who rides away and starts again elsewhere. But I think of Sandra Jean. When we decided to run away to California together—we cancelled our college classes and cashed our chips to pay the way—we were committed, we suffered together that endless bus ride to Berkeley, kept each other safe and steady. Once there she quickly got a job; I didn't, not even washing dishes. We got a barren apartment above a smelly pet shop, furnished (I finally saw) with undersized children's furniture. Too symbolic. The contacts and friends-of-contacts who had invited us to this new land tried to help, took us around, once to a pretty little cabin-cottage near beatnik central. The occupant was a nice and welcoming guy, a folksinger, guitarist, and the younger brother of W. D. Snodgrass, the poet with the absurd name. A nice oriental rug on his floor. When a few days later Sandra Jean chucked me, without apology, to share his place, I could only think it was the rug that won her. I was now near penniless—I had to write the parents, tell the whole sad story, and ask for a plane ticket home.

Today a trip to the Brooklyn Library (the only one I can reach easily from here and get a card from, and that has the kinds of books I seek). Alone now I can spend all the time I want. Wandering yielded a couple of things I didn't know I needed. One was a thick biography of Lord Byron, a person or a personage who's always interested me. His friendship/enmity with Shelley—Byron was among those who burned Shelley's drownd body on the Italian shore. Mary Shelley was more than half in love with B. Reading and pondering this I began to think of a play, a play about poet-brothers who are opposites, in a dance with one another. I'll have to get a new typewriter ribbon. This could take a while, or no time at all. The other book I picked up solely because of the title: *The Art of Memory*. Frances ("Dame" Frances) Yates. Very new—1966 copyright. I had no idea what could be meant by an art of memory and how to do it (or do I actually in effect practice it, and if so how and for what reason anyway?). Mostly dense historical treatments of Renaissance thinkers and painters.

1967

Begun writing the play about Byron and Shelley in Italy. Lots of odd angles and what I'd think of as modernist tricks, but really I'm not familiar with New Theater. There would be a sort of bleachers at the back of the stage; actors seated there would enter the action, speak to Byron, in dialogue tell his life in bits. An elderly man, servant at Byron's father's vast estate. "Haven't known you as a Lord, m'Lord. Back at home we still think of you as wee." "Well so I am, Jock," Byron answers, moved: "Still wee." I think I might be good at this.

This place is vast without L. The cats that should have been hers to take and care for are still here, each with its tics and individuality. Punky still nurses herself on her tiny pink teat—never knew a mother's caresses (sob). Mao is the fiercer, but at evening—this is apparently a ritual in catdom, and I feel sort of privileged to witness it—as evening comes on they begin to get restless, then one chases the other, the other flees, then the first turns on the second and they fly across the room, leaping to every height they can reach (the top of the fridge), then reverse course and race back to the start and face off, snarling in a play-acting fashion—and then they stop. Take their usual places, tuck their paws beneath them and their tails around them, and though on watch briefly they are pretty soon asleep.

It's become clear that I will have to give up this place. L's and my combined incomes hardly covered the rent, and now that's diminished by more than half. And I've failed as a photographer. Ad will appear in the *Voice* rentals columns tomorrow.

Meantime the Children's Crusade keeps on. Returning from another Brooklyn Library trip and coming up out of the subway at Spring Street I entered into a mass of people that hadn't been there this morning. Los Lobos de Lafayette doing a huge business. On the doorstep I find a young man, maybe eighteen, maybe not so old as that. He looked completely exhausted and somewhat bedazzled. Asked if I could help. Some water, he asked. Sure, come on up. When he'd got a little hydrated I asked how far he'd come—from school in Ohio, hitchhiking, then a bus, then a van with others he met with, then alone again, thumb out. And long walking, wearing only a pair of flip-flops. He with the thousands who've come to NYC for the great anti-war march on April 29. We talked about those matters—the war, the government, the deaths, the wrongs done, the fight for peace. He had some papers to present to whatever lawyers or unions he could reach to get an exemption. I sensed us there on an island in a stream, where we—he at least—couldn't stay. I've never spoken or used the word "wistful" but that's what he was. I went and found him an old pair of boots of mine, and socks. Said he could stay a night if he wanted, but he was ready to go on. Something of the saint—or martyr—about him. We agreed to keep a lookout for one another on the great day. Also possibly present, L and Dan—he being so bound up in social change, the war, the government, etc. Often lectured me about it.

Nobody known to me appeared in the astonishingly enormous crowd, or crowds actually, forming up along different streets, west, east, south, moving toward the Park and the Sheep Meadow. From the bottom of the Park you could turn and look back down Fifth Avenue and see the mass extending all the way to Union Square or farther, from where the downtown people formed up, myself among them for a time. I found myself (!) walking beside a group of nuns, arms linked, all singing the *Dona Nobis Pacem* together, and I joined them. It seemed impossible that this outpouring, and all the others like it in every city you could read about (or see on TV if you had such means), could not bring forth a consensus for withdrawing from this foreign war. The weather was asserting the same: as bounteous as any day or days I've ever walked in. Saw no one I knew, but many who looked like people I knew.

Wednesday. Replies to my *Voice* ad. Two young guys, one actually named Byron. They have plans for the space though I'm not sure just what (Art? Photography? Clothes? Dope?). They didn't quail at the figure I set for the work L and I did here—the immovable bed among other things, the sanding job, the bookshelves and the built-in desk where I've been typing my play. I ask $300. No problem sez they. I asked if I could have the place for a further week while I found somewhere else to go. I should be grieving: the career I set out on, now stalled; L gone away; jobs to seek. Somehow it's okay to go. It had been sort of a dream anyway.

At least I won't be homeless: John Foote tells me he's going to England with a woman and is going to be married and study painting. This doesn't fit with what I thought I knew: there was one night we sat up late having a drink in his studio and he said he'd been tempted more than once to make a move my way—but then said that if he did we'd probably both bust out laughing and get nowhere. He's invested in a small brownstone on the Upper West Side. It's in need of some rehab, but if I wanted I could squat in an empty apartment there while he's gone on his month-long honeymoon, maybe longer. I said yes I would take him up on that. No job, no purpose, no friends, no aspirations. That Byron play, almost finished, well a messy draft at least. And another thing I can hardly even begin to describe, far from begun, if it ever is begun.

Rescue a slatted orange crate from the street to put the animals in. A towel in the bottom for comfort. They don't mind, so far; they both like enclosed spaces. A small-load moving company I find advertising in the *East Village Other* arrives and helps me with my small load—clothes in cardboard boxes, books likewise, photographs, typewriter, ½ bottle of Scotch, letters and diary, quilt, dishes and utensils in the last cardboard box. My phone, for which I will still have to pay rent in Foote's place, if I can figure out how to wire it. The box of color slides. Sad, sad.

Meet the contractor who'll be doing John's upgrades. Gives me a couple of keys—the front door, the garden door. His phone number for emergencies. I've been given the basement apartment, which isn't exactly a basement—it has windows on the street, and the kitchen behind has windows on the back garden, not a garden now—an unweeded garden, that grows to seed; things rank and gross in nature do possess it merely, etc. Maybe I could clear it out.

Meantime I unpack or empty out the boxes and crates. The cats wary. Glad I brought food for them. Opened the street window to let out the muggy closed-room air. For a minute I worried about the cats escaping, but then I saw that there was an air-conditioner cage that had been fitted in, the air-conditioner removed. Okay. I got enough from the box I'd filled with foodstuffs (What's the difference between food and foodstuffs?) for dinner, and poured cat food in a dish for the cats. We ate in silence. Early bedtimes for all. I was exhausted, in the original meaning: everything drawn out of me. But still a small sense of ongoingness. How not? The cot that John Foote had brought in while he made plans for renovation, a table too. I will do this. I have no choice.

I had heard the cats making small noises for a bit in the night. Then all quiet. Cars softly passing on West End Avenue. I wept briefly. In the morning I called the cats, shook the box of food, no response. Looked all around. *Kitty kitty kitty.* No cats. Door to the upstairs, to the garden, both shut. In the street window the air-conditioner cage. When I went to see if they could have got out that way somehow I saw that while the cage had three sides and a top, it had no bottom. Which an air conditioner wouldn't need. They'd gone out that way and hadn't returned—no smells they knew to coax them back. I have no cats. I am catless.

Spent much of the morning going from block to block trying to catch a glimpse of one, or allowing them to catch a glimpse of me, but nothing. Apparently I'm to lose everything that has mattered to me. Thoughts of L: that she'd never had an orgasm. Wasn't me, she said; she hadn't *ever* had one, by any method. Yet she seemed to like sex, and liked sex with me, or so I thought. At noon I stopped at a place called the Norwood Café. Old Jewish men reading papers. I got a sandwich and a Coke. Next visit I'll get coffee and read the papers. Went back to the house. Slept. Awakened to hear a mewing or scratching at the door to the basement. Opened it to see a small black cat, looking a bit bewildered and very shabby. *How'd you get in here?* I tried to pet it, and my hand came away black. The animal was *filthy*. I wasn't going to let it into the apartment. I shooed it away back into the basement. Later on I filled a bowl with the food my own cats won't be eating and set it on the top stair of the stairs to the basement and closed the door. All I am willing to do.

Kathy and my sister Jo are living in DC now, Jo in school. The big antiwar march on the Capitol and the Pentagon is in two weeks. I want to go and I don't. The radiance of the NYC march in the sun can't be replicated; I'm peaceful but not a peacenik. The trains and buses will be overwhelmed. Smack shut the journal. No. *[JC will in the end join the million who went to Washington to "confront the warmakers" in an effort at once fatuous and heart-lifting. See below.]*

House hunting. Back to the Lower East Side where once I dwelt. With my *Village Voice* opened to Rentals I walk these streets again, these avenues. (Odd reawakening in me of scenes from *Last Year in Marienbad*, the greatest film I know. Tenements and stickball players and trash in the gutters, as against broad walkways, gushing fountains, men in evening dress, women in gowns. How strange that I can watch those scenes even while walking these mean streets.) Now how about this choice? 270 East 10th Street, only a few buildings in from First Avenue. Okay. In I go. The available apartment is not in the apartment building itself but in a small building behind, where the garden should be. A little metal bridge or walkway goes from the back door of the main building to the little three-story building. The super hands me a key, points the way.

It's tiny. One room, with a toilet built into a corner (surely wasn't there in the past; use the ones in the main building). A kitchen, with sink and tub; the tub having the white enameled cover that makes for a worktable when the tub's not being used. How familiar I am with all these things. A window with panes that are opened outward rather than lifted upward. And a branch of the universal East Side backyard tree: Stinkweed, some call it, but also Tree of Heaven or "Chinese" Something or *Ailanthus*. Its branches reaching in through the window as though taking a look. Charming, it might be called. Anyway the rent is forty-eight dollars a month, and all of me can fit inside it. Quickly I make a deal with the super, plus a fiver, sign a thing, write a check, and get a key. How easy that was. To celebrate I walk uptown and go into Max's Kansas City, the hip artist/rockstar restaurant-bar that opened a year or so before and is now famed. Lou Reed and any number of Warhol epigones can be met with. What I love about it is that the name that's spread across the front is cast in "Cooper Black," a font my old art-department guy liked to use; it has a sort of cowboy/saloon feel, and the careful choice endears the place to me.

It was five o'clock, and I could get a beer without being shunted aside by Debbie Harry or one of the Stooges and their followers.

Nice and cool too. A handsome woman (size large) drinking a glass of white wine. Marcia. We chat. She confesses that she's waiting for the usual crowd to appear, the junkies especially; she confesses a motherly feeling toward junkies. I'm not a junkie but she decides I'm skinny enough to be one. She invites me to her place in the West Village, but I say I have a cat to feed. We exchange phone numbers; she's clear that I can usually meet her here after work (she's in advertising).

[Despite his resistance to the Pentagon event, JC in the end joined the New York contingent and went out with the flag-waving, poster-bearing crowds on the Greyhound bus (the trains were oversold). He brought his diary/daybook and apparently made notes in "real time," as it was not said then. Need it be described?] Everyone in the world has seen it on television. Even I saw it on television at Jo's D.C. apartment as the event was ramping up. Slept on her floor, and next day entered the effulgent stream. On TV, shot from copters overhead, it had really looked like a stream: flowing this way and that, dividing and merging again, channeled by mounted police, forced into avenues around government buildings, pressed close to armed soldiers awaiting orders. What orders would those be? We feel little alarm or fear, but we know what the powers can and will do to keep their status and control. We march *en masse* and unopposed past the Lincoln Memorial, across Memorial Bridge and all the way to the front steps of the Pentagon. Here Abbie Hoffman and the Yippies are pumping up to levitate the building. "We will dye the Potomac red," his handouts said. "Burn the cherry trees, panhandle embassies, attack with water pistols, marbles, bubble gum wrappers, bazookas, girls will run naked and piss on the Pentagon

walls." I didn't know that "Yippy" stood for Youth International Party, and likely many others didn't either. "We shall raise the flag of nothingness over the Pentagon," the Party claimed, "and a mighty cheer of liberation will echo through the land!" I found myself (!) on a flight of steps guarded by helmeted MPs, where we males in a sort of crazed courage burned our draft cards with cigarette lighters as the women cheered us (another crime committed!). My precious IVF went up, a tiny momentary flame in the dull day. I will have to apply for a new issue; I can't be without it and feel safe: I had been instructed to keep it on my person at all times. The Pentagon trembled briefly, like a monster in a cave (I felt the tremor, yes I did, but not what caused it, what divinity or dynamo). Then the long dispersal.

Back home on the train, standing most of the way. By the time I reached the Foote place, I could tell that I had acquired a cold. I opened the basement door and put out the kibble (what is the awful burnt smell that comes up from down there?) and called *Kitty kitty* and up it comes, still expecting to get in. Nope. What'll I do with it when I leave for downtown? Getting unsteady, shaky. Fierce headache. Run a tub of hot water and smoke a joint while it fills. Dig out that bottle of Scotch I brought here and poured a small glassful, let myself down into the tub. This was delightful, maybe therapeutic (son of a doctor, but learned nothing about treatments for anything). When the water began to cool I clambered out and nearly fell over. I'd turned to rubber. The triple treatment! I was laughing in glee while my physical self kept threatening collapse. Then to bed. Tomorrow to fresh woods, and pastures new.

I've called the building manager and told him where I'm leaving the keys. I got the same van and driver coming today to bring me to my new little bolt-hole in a far part of the city. Then, having packed up the last of my stuff in readiness, I went to the door of the basement, opened it, intending to put the remainder of the Kitty Chow where the cat could reach it (in a hubcap I'd picked up in the street, in fact). But as soon as the door was opened, and almost before I called, I saw it hustling up the stairs. I flicked on the light and could see what I hadn't before: white patches showing through the filth. It couldn't be so—but it was. My cat, Punky. I picked her up and took her to the sink, turned on the water, and with her struggling I washed her. The black came off. Underneath it was her: same markings, same tummy with its teats. How on earth she got back into the house, into the basement, how she'd got so filthy . . . but then that bad burnt-oil smell, and the building manager saying to me to watch out for the furnace (there being of course nothing I could "watch out" about), but maybe it had exploded, put out some fart or puff of black smoke that coated her. I'll never know. I wrapped her in a towel; she was shivering violently—as violently as such a small package could—and I held her in my lap and laughed. On the trip downtown in the van, I tried to tell the driver the amazing tale but he was only half listening. He gave me a hand unloading at 270 East 10th, and I gave him another five from Byron's $300, which won't last much further. I'll need a bed. A narrow bed.

Meanwhile something has happened, or is happening, in the writing of this diary or whatever it is. From the news I read passages of ordinary events (which everyone knows and no one in the future will care about) and enter them in my own pages, and when I pick up the journal later and look through these late entries I find that more than one of them was written in a future tense. *I will be at the October March on Washington*, I did not write. *A village in a Viet Cong area is to be bombed and incinerated with napalm.* Why did I think I knew anything of that? I know nothing. What is this page? Was I stoned? I wish. As though the book, *Record* its name, is rather a commandment, an order: *Record!* But what?

Yet what return to me now are dim but definite scenes that connect to nothing else, like frames from ancient black-and-white movies. How was it that L and I had a last meeting, a farewell, sitting in the cold on a bench in the forecourt of a gloomy mansion, now the offices of some social enterprise? She was dressed not in her bunny-fur but in a dark brown felted coat of some sort; she told me she was going back to California, that Dan had gone back to his wife and kids. I recorded it, but did it happen?

And how then could it be that Dan came to John Foote's building when I was sick in bed, pushed open the downstairs door, which I hadn't locked? I am certain that by then I had moved up to the bedroom on the second floor, as the building manager had asked me to do, because he had work to do in the kitchen below. Had Dan called on the phone, had he come to the door? Anyway there I was in bed, and Dan—I can see him still, rising up the stairs, hear him call to me, and the feeling of rage and disgust. Trying to tell me something about L or his own business, that he knew I'd gone to his wife's place, and how he didn't hold it against me that I'd had sex with her, and I told him with all the voice I could summon, to *go*, get the *fuck out of here, go away*, now weeping as well as choking and drowning in snot. And at last he turned and went.

But did that happen, that I went to his wife's apartment some days before, met their kids (four and five), she a mild and clearly a good person, giving the boys their baths; and we talked about Dan and L and South Bend and all that had happened; and did I really go to bed with her as some sort of payback, that she was okay with it, and we made more love than sex, and in mutual sorrow? And how then could it be that in some room in some apartment, years later, L and I met, and she told me how she'd taken LSD or some other psychedelic in California, and had her first orgasm; how she laughed and said it didn't seem that big a deal. These dreamlike things that I must believe were real.

1968

My uptown drug dealer, near where John Foote's building was, and where JanR and her now longtime boyfriend, Yeu-Bun Yee, have an apartment. A fine photographer with a spinal curvature that makes him about the size of a child of twelve (Jan is still tall). The dealer is somewhat creepy and always flush with weed. But on this night when I got there a dreadful thing—dreadful to me—occurs. Difficult if not impossible to describe. Pot, the innocent pot, pot that knits up the raveled sleeve of care, balm of hurt minds: it turned demonic on me. After he'd counted out what I'd asked for and taken my money, he picked up a rolled joint and lit it. Offered it to me with what in retrospect seems a malicious grin. *Very strong stuff*, he avers. We had been talking about Nabokov; his feelings that N was a cold-hearted man with a cold mind. I conceded that he could be read as cold, but not *Lolita*, so full of profound pathos. I take a hit, he takes a hit, I take another. Time to go. Beginning to feel quite strange. Once out into the night, on the street, still thinking of Nabokov, of pathos and coldness, and a thing forms in my mind, or two things: something warm and mammalian, and something avian, all eyes and spiky hardness, like a parrot. They begin to crash into one another, planets soft and glassy-hard destroying each other as they rush together in terrified slow-motion and silence. And a voice—but no voice—seems to call me: *Now do you see? Now do you understand? You haven't known but now you do: you get it now, don't you.* It seemed to be not within me but in the night sky, a lesson, a vision—I can't describe it further except that it was destroying itself and me and the supports of the world, all in utter silence.

Walked back to Jan and Yeu-Bun's, almost unable to speak. Bun, after hearing the story, said wow, what an experience! Like some psychedelic hit. Had it contained DMT? Was it that? I couldn't think. Why would an inexpensive drug—pot—have an expensive additive put in it, what seller would do that? They sat me down, gave me wine, played a recording of Satie pieces. Things to grasp and keep me afloat. Left at last and went back downtown, almost unable to find my way to 270 East 10th. Now this morning trying to write about it, impossible. About noon I took out some of the stuff I got from the dealer and very carefully tried a puff or two. And immediately the experience of last night returned—or rather I became terrified that it might return. I think of people condemned to death (Dostoevsky, e.g.) who are lined up blindfolded to be shot, who hear the guns fired, but aren't killed. Blanks, fired merely to terrify. In a way they *are* killed: can't ever get entirely away from the lineup. I may not be able to smoke any longer: I'm actually afraid of it.

Gone to see my friend Marcia, the one I met at Max's on an empty afternoon. I need her now, and I like her a lot. Far away from the sort of woman I'd choose, if a choice were offered, but those aren't offered. She's generous, she laughs a lot, she laughs at herself, but is easily touched. I wrote out for her a bit of something I'd thought of: *The Things that Make Us Happy Make Us Wise.* She was moved by this; she'd lay it out on a child's tablet, she said, with a child's printed letters. And she looks at me as though I'm an innocent soul to have thought this up.

The job she just got in an advertising bureau—she's discovered, pretty quickly, that the CEO is afflicted with uncontrollable tics and speech—the condition she says is Tourette's syndrome, something I'd never heard of. He crunches up, lifts a knee, makes noises, yells out stuff—his commonest remark is *Pull my tie!*, which so far she's avoided doing. She was between horrified and feeling for him, and she's learned he's really smart. She was going to pass on the job, but the money was very good (maybe he has a hard time attracting help—it's a small agency), and she felt bad about just walking away. Her place is comfy and upholstered but a little dark—somehow the sun can't come in direct on any side. First night with her worked out pretty well—some laughter, some seeking what works, etc. It's good. A good bed, too—but she says she can't sleep with another in the bed—so I'm sent to the small guest bedroom. A guest is what I am. It's fine. I have a friend. A large Jewish friend. I invite her to my place, where at the moment there is no bed at all—not that she'd spend the night here in any case. "Salvation Army," she says. "They've got everything. Beds, chairs, stuff. Pots and pans." I think she thinks I'm poor. I *am* poor. She's thinking of moving to Florida before winter comes and starting anew. Coral Gables. Somehow in the weeks when I didn't see her she acquired a large tortoise; she'd expected it to wander around the place, granting its aliveness to the rug and the linoleum. But something—perhaps an instinct for hibernation—drives him under the couch, where he lies unmoving for days. When she goes South she'll take him, she says, and let him go in the sun and the sand.

She's right about the Salvation Army. A thin but seemingly unused mattress wrapped in plastic, somewhat wider than a single but not quite a double, five dollars. A lamp. A desk for a child in middle school, now for me, a graduate, in cheap wood and pressboard but sturdy. All these things to be delivered to my building in the white truck with the red badge on it. Five dollars for the service. This really is the end of Byron's (the human's) three hundred: I need more money. From a Japanese store in the West Village I get a comforter, amazingly cheap, like a sheet and a blanket in one. Not large like the bedding at 236 Lafayette but wide enough for the monastic board that for a while I'll be sleeping on. And two matching pillows. I'll sleep on the floor like Toshiro Mifune in *Sanjuro*. The demonic struggle that night at Joe's building up on the West Side still comes over me. Even the sweet smell of it on the street. I'll drink from my Scotch bottle and avoid the weed.

[Late in the year, Lance Bird and Betsy were married in a very small wedding in a friend's apartment; the celebrant was Sidney Lanier, director of the American Place Theater, friend and distant cousin of Tennessee Williams. JC read a poem he had written for the occasion. Bird had got Lanier's attention and was planning to bring JC's play about Byron to him. JC attended the wedding with Marcia.]

So the American Place Theater, to which I'd submitted the Byron play some weeks ago, has reluctantly (I really believe that Sidney Lanier was reluctant) turned it down. Sidney was full of praise, but if I have learned anything (likely I have not), it's that there are far more plans and submissions in this realm than there are producers with power, taste, and money, and that praise, interest, encouragement, and fellowship are coin that can't be spent. Maybe I could turn it into a novel; Lance was deeply moved by it when he read the first draft and was sure it would make a great film.

1969

Strangely warm weather for November. Tonight the temp at 9 o'clock is 82. What's going to bring in the ice storms? Only six weeks till the page turns for good: the new four reversible or upside-down digits, hard to believe in: like living in the future, or far away. The daybook I began with, which was large enough to hold not only the Sixties but some part of the unknowable decade already forming in the breast of time, has begun falling apart for no reason I can tell. Leaves drop out when the book is opened, and I see that the writing fades, as though left in sun or rain. Some have already been lost. *As the generation of leaves, so is that of men.* I feel myself on these hot autumn days, when the city stinks, to be on the point of dissolution. Where are the moments that I recounted there? I leaf through the pages and don't see what I put down. I make errors in going to and from places that I have walked in this city now for years, certain I am wrong and not knowing what would be right.

But I have a new job, taken in preference to starving or despair. I got the invitation, if that's the term, in the *East Village Other*: the New York Telephone Company is hiring fact-checkers for a new edition of the Manhattan telephone book. The ad was full of drug references and hippie language—why would that be? Maybe the pay would be worse than for fact-checking tax returns, which I did for a few nights some time ago. Anyway, I go up to the West Forties and this office, unconnected physically to the home office, and yes, the workers are a pretty hairy and happy bunch. The work's easy but tedious. The NyTel is switching to a "computerized" telephone book, and the job is to check the new computer's listings against the old printed sheets. These two issues are named the Photon (the computer-printed) and the Metal (for the old-fashioned printing plates used for decades in the past). What's wanted is to find where the Photon pages are wrong compared to the Metal. And almost immediately it is evident that the Photon is at a loss. The two are put before the worker side by side, and a magnifying bar (to avoid misreadings) is slid down over both entries, and the Photon is marked when in error, which it commonly is; sometimes whole pages are wrong, multiple listings of the same name or business. Why do I find all this somehow joyful? I have a rough map of Manhattan in my brain, its neighborhoods and their qualities, and I can sort of place the people whose names and addresses I read. When I walk those streets and neighborhoods, I feel I know the inhabitants in a special way. I'm not only proofing the pages, the names and numbers; I am reading the book. And what book could come closer to being called the Book of Life? Life is all that it contains. As soon as they're known about, the dead inhabiting it are made to depart. *[This operation of New York Telephone has been impossible to track down in the archives. Information about it must exist, but the evanescence that seems to have carried it off leaves only JC's memories of it as facts of a kind. It's quite possible that this—and not only this—episode in the New York years is actually a* jeu d'esprit, *as the far stranger evolutions to come in this daybook might also be.]*

The proofreaders come and go—some of them find the tedium exasperating—but some like me adapt and come to find it bearable; there are jobs in this city that are far less bearable. One who is both amiable and hard-working is a young Puerto Rican woman—at least I assume she's Puerto Rican, through the slight olive cast to her skin, which glows faintly under the fluorescents. Long glossy black hair, a sweet low laugh. As the shop was closing yesterday (a Friday), another young Puerto Rican woman came into the shop and sat with Lori and talked earnestly for a long time. Obviously in trouble or in a quandary. I asked what it was about (me being an authority here, and the shop closing soon). It appears that the new person—M is what I'll name her—has nowhere to stay tonight. Boyfriend's got the only key and he's gone away. *Un guillao* she calls him with a dismissive flip of a hand. *Incordio*. Lori: Did I know anyone among the gang here who might have a space? She wouldn't take up much room. Well—I scanned the departing crew and couldn't think which if any would be all right with this young person (eighteen, I'd soon learn). Not as delicately beautiful as her sister—skin a bright brown with rose highlights—angry and aboil just now, seeking solution. I said . . . well of course I said—I'd be happy to put you up, but my place is small. Like, tiny. She gives me a hug, problem solved. We take the train downtown, walk from Union Square. Takes my arm. Charmed by the bridge to my little building, by my cat, by the bed on the floor. *You sleep on the FLAW?* She tells me more about herself and her loves and family; cries a little. I'd said she could have a place here, but I hadn't said what the circumstances might be: one bed for two, unless one sleeps on the floor beside the bed. There's really no place to sit side by side. Pretty soon we are not sitting. She's pleased with me, I think: not just for the charity extended.

Sunday. M vanishes for a day or a night and reappears unchanged, laughing, shameless, but not quite as real as before. She's been up to the Bronx to make sure her family's okay. Why not okay? Maybe to see if the old boyfriend is back and his door open. Wants to get her birth certificate, some secret money, her mother's address—she's in an asylum upstate. We are both children, neither of us the older, neither of us settled. We know so little; we know nothing. M listening to the radio, a salsa station. She tries to teach me to dance salsa: hopeless. Am I in her world, or is she in mine?

My father is dead: a telegram, the first I've seen in years, and the last ever. M cuts my hair, so that I am respectable, cutting, clipping, sharing my tears. I believe or seem to believe I have no way to get home; letters take weeks now. The vascular problem he died of might descend to me, I am somehow sure of this, but I know also that it will be decades till I know in fact. *[JC did much later undergo open-heart surgery for repair of the failing aorta that was the cause of his father's sudden death in the hospital awaiting an X-ray.]*

Police cars roam the neighborhood, making noise like giants' speech. I have lost the pen that I began the daybook with. What would it be like if now I could talk to Dad, now where he is, tell him about myself at last, without shame or avoidance. Eyes I dare not meet in dreams, in Death's dream kingdom. I do dare. I'll walk if I have to, if I can. Somewhere or somewhere else I will find an opening and step out into a place or time I have never seen but know. I have good boots and I can study the stars, so long as they keep their places. Others wiser than me are gone on ahead, I'm sure of it, it's reported. Ask M to come with me, and she sheds tears anew, all she has for me in the way of love and refusal.

High-rise apartment buildings are being abandoned: the grid can't hold. What does that mean, the grid? The Cuyahoga River in Ohio has caught fire. In parts of New York the phones are failing, or at least losing clarity; people can't understand each other. *There must be a knot in the cord,* they say. People are walking, carrying their children, cars left behind, no gas—why not? But weren't those cities always partially imaginary to you if you'd never passed through them? If you follow the banks of a channeled river does it flow out through the world at last, cleaning itself as it passes through open lands and wooded places, and can it bypass the next smoky city and the next? Acid rain destroys shirts and sheets hung out on the roofs of buildings; small airplanes fly through the acid fog, collecting samples of the truth. I am like a child of twelve. Do all the soldiers who are coming home feel glad? In a few days, with the daybook, with all my money but the rent in an envelope for M to hand on. *Ay papi*, she said, coupled on our bed at morning. *Ay Papi yo vengo.* Not meaning that she'll come with me where I must go. And so with the little cat in the pocket of my old overcoat, I'll go. Walk up the narrow island until a bridge is reached. Stand beside four-lane highways, feeling the blow of passing trucks and cars, of trucks carrying cars. People carry small radios, hold them up to the sky to get a signal: the same people as those I photographed for the Radio Bureau.

Astonishing litter along the highway and along each side, one the northward-going side, the other the southward side: those going forward, those returning in hopeless hope. I have never driven a car. It amazes me that the wide roads where the great trucks and all the cars and vans went now unfold in what seems to be untouched wild land. Is it because there are no human things along them, these great gray highways, no houses and gardens and churches, no car can leave this road and enter a driveway where a screen door opens, a woman steps out. No. Passing through. The same thing always. We late travelers sort through the trash and argue over food, money flung away by those in despair, useless to them, gone, who knows where by now, not even the radio people know. I am certain that the small bedraggled woman younger than she looks, searching without purpose, is the mother of Lori and M, escaped or let go from the asylum; she speaks to others in Puerto Rican Spanish and they shrug and move away. I try to reach her, to say her children are well, but she has vanished.

Tall clouds forming in the north to which we go. Evening comes and small fires are started; some small groups gather, sit on the outskirts of their circles, tell to others how they came out from the midlands well before the collapse, and carry with them not only things but thoughts; they speak to one another and touch the shoulders of friends. What do they talk about? About the different kinds of persons there are, about what in the world of thought and desire is appropriate to this sort of person, but not to that; what this kind is good at, and what not. I learn that in days not weeks we will break through the forests and it will be Vermont, if it's still there. I will pass from them then, the walkers, knowing now my way, and solitary. My mother is waiting for me without the slightest hope that I'll come, but I will come. Blue-green the foliage in high summer. Here is the church, here is the steeple; open the doors and see all the people. He lies in the aisle before the altar; I think, How can he breathe, closed up in that box? My mother and sisters are there, myself unrecognizable to them for a moment. One by one I embrace them. *I will look up unto the hills, the hills whence cometh my help,* says the priest. Where we stand at the sharply squared hole we can look to Ascutney in the south, blue and faded. When a night and a day have come and passed I will turn back, they'll want me to stay here in the unchanged land, but I must go back, my thought runs back not forward: thought's the slave of life, and life's time's fool, and time, that takes survey of all the world, must have a stop. I'll go back toward where I live if I can, in this blue weather, what my mother calls injun summer.

And I am at my desk again now at 270 East 10th Street. It's hot. M is asleep wrapped in a sheet and nothing more. The cat I bore so far and long, the cat L took from the street in the imaginary past, is in the bed with her. I am afraid of dreaming. Tomorrow I'll return again to reading the names and telephone numbers of those who have already abandoned the city and gone on ahead, whom I can see as well as I can see the typed papers that are accumulating under my left hand. So many, I had not thought death had undone so many.

There are some two hundred names in the book that start with Z, and when all of them are corrected or passed by our checking we will have a stop and we will leave, though the bosses say we will soon be called back to start again. The other book, the book I think I type at this desk, doesn't exist yet but it is in service of the walkers and what they lost forever, how they must proceed for generations, passing by all that can't be saved or is lost or no longer wanted; they are beyond any knowledge I now possess, going on in trust and in sorrow, sitting in circles to teach and to learn, passing out of what has been and into lost lands and what will be made. Going now into that endless summer, a summer that has come even here. Learning to live with it: I must.

[There is no accounting for these final pages of the daybook begun five years before. What they appear to report can't be reported, because the events can't be matched to what in fact happened in the last year of the decade; what he meant can't now be known with any certainty. He seems unable to understand what he had himself written (in pencil and a blue crayon, after the loss of the pen he had written with for so long). After he returned to New York, he and M moved together to a larger and somewhat grander apartment on Lexington Avenue, and with money from film-writing work he could furnish it with beds and a couch and even a TV. He began a new diary of his experiences through the 1970s: delights, griefs, sins, successes, things shameful and noble. It is now among JC's papers housed at the Harry Ransom Center in Austin, Texas. That diary, which I have been allowed to peruse, is unlikely—due to its contents—to be published in any foreseeable future.]

John Crowley is the author of thirteen novels, including *Little, Big*, the Ægypt series, *Engine Summer*, *Ka: Dar Oakley in the Ruin of Ymr*, and *Flint and Mirror*. He is a three-time winner of the World Fantasy Award, including one for Lifetime Achievement.